A Battle of Wills and Words

A TEATIME TALES
NOVELETTE

LEENIE BROWN

Leenie B Books
Halifax

ISBNs: 978-1-989410-82-0 (ebook); 978-1-990607-15-8 (paperback); 978-1-990607-16-5 (large print edition)

www.leeniebbooks.com

www.leeniebrown.com

Chapter 1

HENRY FITZWILLIAM, EARL MATLOCK, surveyed his table. The candelabras stood regally above the small dishes and the grander displays that decorated the central length. The bright white cloth which covered the mahogany tabletop and draped down its sides held not a crease. The glasses and silver glistened and sparkled just as they should.

His mother, whose portrait hung on the wall behind his wife and opposite of him, would be proud of such a table as this, and that knowledge puffed up Henry's pride of position as master of all that lay before him much more than any spectacular marzipan creation or perfectly cooked morsel of food ever could.

Family had been of utmost importance to his mother and father, and he strove, as best he knew how, to continue that tradition within his domain. His youngest sister, Anne, had been exceptionally good at creating the sort of family their mother had aspired to preside over. His other sister, Catherine, had been far less successful.

While Anne nurtured love, Catherine encouraged loftiness. Duty to one's station, increasing standing, and being bowed to by all whom she considered beneath her had made her cold. He knew that behind her frosty exterior, she loved her daughter and nieces and nephews. It was simply that she had blessed little understanding of how best to communicate that love other than through attempting to arrange advantageous friendships and reminding each of the younger generation about their good fortune in being born into the family of the Earl of Matlock.

Catherine was the reason for this evening's soiree, for she had come to visit Henry three weeks ago in quite a state of agitation, fuming and sputtering about a fortune-hunting adventurous of little standing who had bewitched their nephew and their sister Anne's only son, Fitzwilliam Darcy.

Henry had done his best to assure her that Darcy was not one to fall prey to a fool. He drew and released a breath as he took up his wine glass. Catherine, of course, had deemed it necessary to remind him of the recent, unfortunate incident involving Darcy's younger sister and the companion who led the child astray and nearly into the clutches of a true fortune-hunting cad.

Henry had reminded her that neither he nor Lady Matlock had found any reason to question Darcy's choice to employ Mrs. Younge. Still, Catherine was not without a point. Men just as good and noble as Darcy had fallen for ladies who loved their wealth and position more than they loved the man to whom they were tying themselves. Such a thing might be acceptable in some families, but not in one which would hold true to the Fitzwilliam tradition of forming firm and loving bonds between family members.

From the glances and smiles he had witnessed pass between Darcy and his betrothed during the many courses of their meal, Henry had very little doubt that the two young people were madly smitten with one another. Of course, that information would not be welcomed by Catherine. To put it mildly, his sister was not good at accepting the fact that she could be wrong.

"Ladies, shall we retire to the drawing room?"

Lady Matlock stood, and Henry followed suit and remained standing until there were only men left at the table. Then, he retook his place, though in a more relaxed posture. The most formal portion of the evening was over. His staff and guests had all performed their parts well thus far. He had seen enough to know that Miss Elizabeth Bennet was equal to the challenge of precise and proper decorum as would well befit her role as Mrs. Darcy. The remainder of the evening would be an evaluation of the lady's ability to engage in conversation and add to it. Darcy needed a wife who was not as reserved as he was and who was intelligent and quick. All indications pointed to Miss Elizabeth being such a lady, but the informality of the drawing room after dinner, when games might be played, would be where firm conclusions could be drawn.

"Mr. Gardiner, would you care for something other than port? I have a selection of libations," Henry offered.

"I am quite content with port, my lord. It is of a high quality." He smiled broadly. "I stock it on occasion in my own cabinet."

"Do you?" Henry eyed the younger man. If he had to guess, Gardiner was not more than thirty-five. From the way the man was dressed and the fact that he knew this particular port, there was no denying that Darcy's description of Gardiner as successful in his trade was no exaggeration.

"Indeed, I do." Mr. Gardiner took a sip of his port, and then, after replacing his glass on the table, he leaned forward and turned his full attention on Lord Matlock. "Does she pass?"

The man was certainly direct. Henry glanced at Darcy, who was looking at him with an intensity in his eyes that was equal to Gardiner's.

"I do not attend balls at Almack's, my lord, but I do have my connections in your realm. I know that my niece does not appear to be an appropriate choice if one is desiring to advance himself in standing, line his coffers, or add to his land holdings. I do not fault you for doing your duty and examining her appropriateness for your nephew. I assure you I have done the same with your nephew."

Darcy's eyes shifted from Henry to Mr. Gardiner, causing Lord Matlock to chuckle. "Does he pass?"

"More than you will likely ever know."

Gardiner shared a meaningful look with Darcy which did nothing to quell Henry's curiosity about whatever had happened that was not being shared.

"I wish I had done more," Darcy said, "sooner."

"Lizzy attempted to prevent it."

Darcy nodded his acceptance and said no more.

Henry shot a questioning look at his youngest son, who merely shrugged. Henry tipped his head in Darcy's direction and his son nodded. Richard would uncover the story. There was not a gentleman in all of England who was as curious and persistent as Richard.

"Does she pass?" Mr. Gardiner repeated.

"I have seen nothing to make me question her fondness for Darcy."

"Nor will you," Darcy muttered.

"I believe she will make you incredibly happy, Darcy. However, I do still hold some reservations about her taking on the role of your wife as it relates to society."

"Your fears are for naught," Gardiner said. "Elizabeth possesses a quick mind and courage that rarely quivers. I believe the ladies of the ton will find her a rather fearsome opponent."

"Do you agree, son?" Henry directed the question to Richard. "You spent time with her at Rosings. Would you agree with her uncle's assessment?"

Richard's head tipped and his brow furrowed as he contemplated the question. "She stood her own against Aunt Catherine, and I would agree that she has a mind that is lively and quick. However, I cannot say with any great certainty that she will be able to survive the ladies of the ton."

"She outwitted Miss Bingley more than once," Darcy inserted.

"Miss Bingley?" Richard laughed. "Caroline only aspires to be as catty as some of the ladies of the ton are."

Darcy shook his head. "You did not see her at Netherfield."

Richard cocked a brow in disbelief.

"She was cruel," Gardiner said. "Jealousy hones those skills quickly."

Richard shook his head. "I will still reserve my judgment on such a thing. Miss Elizabeth is too kind to be cunning."

Mr. Gardiner took another sip of his port and smiled. "Lizzy has four sisters. I promise you that she can be cunning, though usually not unwisely so." Again, the man shared a speaking look with Darcy.

Yes, he would need Richard to discover whatever it was which was being hidden, for it seemed as if it would be quite an interesting story.

"There is nothing else to cause you to withhold your blessing from this union?" Gardiner smiled when Henry looked in his direction. "A deal cannot be completed on vague terms or mere hope. I did not gain my wealth by dreaming it would happen."

Lord Matlock chuckled. "No, I have not found anything else to question, and even with this one question in mind, I would not dare come between Darcy and the lady he has chosen."

Gardiner emptied his glass. "That is noble, my lord, but we all know that tensions within are not good for the fabric of the family."

"You speak truthfully and directly, Gardiner. I like that."

"Then, you will come to love my niece." Amusement danced in Gardiner's eyes. "She is not given to prevarication. Your nephew and my niece are well-matched. There will be times of disagreement between them, but I have negotiated with both enough to know that they will work through the issues satisfactorily."

"You have negotiated with Darcy?"

Gardiner nodded.

"When?" Henry pressed. Perhaps he would not need to wait until later to discover some of the information he longed to know.

"Elizabeth's youngest sister is now Mrs. Wickham," Mr. Gardiner said.

Henry's eyes sifted to Richard, who looked as startled as Henry felt, and then, to Darcy.

"She had no brother to prevent an elopement," Gardiner said.

Henry darted a look toward Gardiner. Apparently, that gentleman knew about Darcy's sister's near elopement with Mr. Wickham.

"I wanted to be part of the financial arrangements for Mr. Wickham, but Mr. Darcy prevented me. Not that I acquiesced readily. However, instead of doing as I wished to do, I was left with the recognition for something I did not do."

And from the tone of displeasure in his voice, Gardiner was still not happy about that.

"What financial arrangements?" Richard asked.

"A commission, his debts, and something to settle on Elizabeth's sister," Darcy answered.

"All of which I could have done," Gardiner grumbled.

Richard whistled, low and slow. "That would be no insignificant amount."

"It was not, and no one is to know that it was me," Darcy said.

"You are keeping a secret from your betrothed?" Richard asked.

Darcy shook his head. "She deciphered the truth when she heard I was at the wedding."

"You were at the wedding?" That was surprising. Henry would not have thought Darcy would have allowed Wickham to know about his involvement.

"I found them at Mrs. Younge's. There was no option but for them to marry, and I wanted to see that it was done." Darcy placed his empty glass on the table. "My only hope for Mrs. Wickham's happiness lies with her husband's demise on the battlefield."

"On this, we agree," Gardiner said. "Lydia is like her mother, but her lot will be a much harder life than my sister's ever was. Mrs. Bennet married a good man, who loves her. He is a bit more at ease than I would like, but Bennet has always cared well for Fanny and his daughters, save when it comes to their futures. Their dowries are not as great as I would like," he clarified.

"I suppose that only matters if they do not choose well when offers are made," Henry said.

Gardiner sighed. "I suppose that is true. They are not fortune hunters, or, at least, the eldest are not, nor does it appear that the youngest was, although that may only be because Lydia does not understand finances as she should. But that is neither here nor there. Elizabeth is not lacking. However, her mother will expect some influence on possible matches for her two remaining daughters – not just from Mr. Darcy, but also from Mr. Bingley. After all, what good is there in her eldest two daughters marrying so well if they cannot help their sisters, and I know that, while Miss Lydia will offer to assist with matching them to officers, Bennet will not hear of that. These facts are perhaps the biggest marks against my niece's match with Mr. Darcy."

"They are not insurmountable," Darcy said. "I am happy to host Elizabeth's sisters when needed."

"Happy to host?" Richard scoffed. "Love has changed him, Father."

Lord Matlock chuckled. "It often does change a man. Your turn is coming, Son."

Richard shook his head and rose from his place. "I do not plan to marry. At least, I do not plan to marry before the viscount. He is the one who needs to produce an heir."

It was always the same with Richard. He always found some reason to put off the idea of marriage. However, his day would come. A gentleman could not be so charming and well-connected as Richard without eventually succumbing to one of the many ladies who buzzed about hoping to snare him. Added to that was the fact that he wore the uniform of a colonel quite well.

"Do you not think we should join the ladies?" Richard asked.

"I do believe that would be an excellent thing to do."

"It will be the best way to come to a determination of Miss Elizabeth's ability to withstand the ton," Richard added.

"You are not to provoke her," Darcy growled.

"I cannot promise anything. We are to be family. Therefore, it stands to reason that she should know the sort of family she is joining."

"Do not besmirch the Fitzwilliam name," Lord Matlock cautioned.

"I can remain at Pemberley all year. I do not need to return to town." Darcy muttered, which only caused Richard to chuckle at Darcy's threat to cut himself off from the family.

"Are they always like this?" Mr. Gardiner asked.

"Like what?" Lord Matlock asked as he and Gardiner followed Darcy and Richard down the hall.

"Taunting each other as brothers might do."

"I fear they are."

"That is good," Gardiner said with satisfaction.

"How is it good?"

"It means your family bonds are strong, and that fact is important for me to feel completely at ease, knowing that Elizabeth will be in such a situation."

"My sister Catherine will be the issue."

"Sisters are often the issue," Gardiner quipped.

Though the man was not old, he bore the wisdom of years in his outlook, and Matlock suspected that would make Darcy and Gardiner good friends. Despite what Catherine might think and his own trepidation about how Darcy's betrothed would deal with the ton, this match between Darcy and Miss Elizabeth seemed to be a good one.

Chapter 2

As he approached the drawing room, Henry could hear the hum of female voices. It sounded as if the ladies were getting on well. From the door, he searched the room for his wife. It was she to whom he always looked first. Her posture would tell him if the situation into which he walked required care or not. She smiled at him and gave a small nod of her head. Her shoulders were not tight, and her hands rested lightly on her lap. All was well. That was a good sign indeed.

His gaze shifted from his wife to his soon-to-be niece. She was turned toward Darcy and smiling. The look was very reminiscent of how his wife always looked so pleased to see him. The affection between Darcy and Miss Elizabeth was not feigned and likely just as unbreakable as the affection that bound him to his wife. He hoped, with all that was in him, that what Gardiner said about the ferocity of Miss Elizabeth's fortitude was true because she seemed to be a lovely young woman. He would hate to see her injured by some backbiting biddy.

"Miss Elizabeth, you simply must tell us about my cousin's proposal." Amelia, Henry's youngest, was a romantic from the top of her bonnet to the bottom of her slippers. Of course, she would wish to know all the sigh-worthy details about her cousin's relationship. However, she was bright enough to know she would not get those details from Darcy.

Miss Elizabeth glanced at Amelia, but her eyes quickly returned to Darcy. Amusement shone in them, and her left eyebrow arched. It appeared she knew how much the telling of such a tale would make him uncomfortable.

"Which one?"

Darcy stopped his progression of crossing the room to sit next to her. The other voices in the room faded to silence. Miss Elizabeth's eyes grew wide, and she leaned towards her sister. Henry moved around his nephew and towards his seat with curiosity nipping at his heels the whole way.

"Did I say that out loud?" she asked softly.

"I am afraid you did," her sister replied.

Miss Elizabeth's eyes closed, and her cheeks grew rosy with what Henry guessed was mortification. How greatly he wanted to ask the meaning of Miss Elizabeth's question!

"You most certainly did." Richard was looking excessively amused by this turn of events.

"Son," Henry cautioned in a low tone as he shook his head to discourage Richard from going where he, himself, wished to go but would not.

As was his normal wont when tormenting his siblings or cousins, Richard ignored the mild scold from his father and continued on his chosen path.

"I, for one, would love to hear about all of them." Richard chuckled. "It seems you have an eager audience waiting to hear your tale. Is that not right, Leelee?"

Amelia pulled her bottom lip between her teeth as she hesitantly nodded her agreement with her brother.

"It is a dreadfully dull tale," Miss Elizabeth replied.

"Oh, but you must tell us something to assuage our curiosity," Richard said as he retrieved the chair from the writing desk and placed it directly in front of Miss Elizabeth before seating himself on it. "I assure you that I will not stop until I have heard the full story. Is that not so, Darcy?"

Miss Elizabeth looked at Darcy, who was just seating himself beside her. His grimace must have been answer enough, for very quickly, she turned back to Richard and asked, "Would you prefer to hear about your cousin's proposal or Mr. Collins's proposal?"

Was that a hint of hopefulness in her voice? She was covering something, and if Henry knew it, so did Richard. However, Lord Matlock had to admire the quickness of her mind in its attempt to turn the situation so neatly.

"Mr. Collins?" Richard's features were suffused with surprise.

The name sounded familiar. Where had he heard it?

"Mr. Collins?" Richard repeated. "Aunt Catherine's parson?"

Ah! Yes! That was where Henry had heard it. His sister had cited the man as the source of the gossip regarding Miss Elizabeth being engaged to Darcy.

"Yes, Colonel, the very same," Miss Elizabeth replied.

Richard settled back in his chair and folded his arms across his chest. "I most certainly would like to hear about that."

"Why would my sister's parson propose to Miss Elizabeth?" Henry asked. "According to Catherine, the man is married."

"Recently married," Richard tossed over his shoulder to his father.

"Mr. Collins is both our cousin and our father's heir," Miss Bennet answered. She had such a sweetness about her, and she was a beauty. He imagined she could calm most situations with a quiet word and a soft smile. However, no amount of serenity would calm Richard's inquisitiveness. Only the revealing of a secret would assuage that.

"He is the heir to your father's estate, you say?" Lord Matlock tilted his head and peered a bit closer at Miss Elizabeth. There must be an entail. Her marrying Mr. Collins would be seen by some to be a great advantage to the family.

"Yes, my lord, Longbourn is entailed, and since my father has no sons, the estate will one day belong to Mr. Collins," Miss Elizabeth explained. "It seems that, upon installing my cousin as her parson, your sister, Lady Catherine, suggested that he find a wife and instructed him that choosing one of his cousins would be an excellent idea."

That most certainly sounded like his sister Catherine. She would be amongst those who would see the match between heir and daughter as advantageous.

Miss Elizabeth smiled wryly. "Within moments of his arrival at Longbourn, he settled in his mind that Jane would be his best choice. However, he was soon disabused of that notion since Jane's heart seemed to be engaged elsewhere. Therefore, he quite naturally decided that the second daughter would be just as good a choice as the first daughter."

"That does sound logical," Lord Matlock said.

Richard snorted with laughter. "Father, have you met Aunt Catherine's parson?"

"No, I have not."

"Logical is not a word I would use to describe the man. He holds Aunt Catherine in high esteem, and before you tell me that such would be expected from a man of Mr. Collins's position, let me add that in his eyes, nothing, and I do mean nothing, she says or does is ever wrong."

"Not a word of contradiction or look of deferred dispute?"

Richard shook his head.

Henry's eyebrows rose. The man must be something to behold if he could pay such homage to a demanding woman such as Catherine was. "I see."

"I do not wish to speak ill of my cousin, for he is family and the husband of a very dear friend," Miss Elizabeth said. "However, I will not hide the truth from you, for I hope that we will also be family soon."

A smile tipped Henry's lips. She placed great value on family. That fact pleased him excessively.

"What the colonel says is true," she continued. "My cousin is not in possession of great wit. In fact, he can be quite insipid at times."

"You must admit, however," Henry said, "that, due to the entail, your marrying this Collins fellow would have been advantageous."

"From the standpoint of property and a secure future, it would have been a very advantageous match."

Henry's eyes shifted for a moment to Mrs. Bennet who muttered something that sounded a great deal like "it most certainly would have been." Apparently, the mother was not pleased the daughter had turned down a marriage of advantage.

"From any other point of view, there is no advantage, for I can assure you that there are not two more unequally matched individuals in this world."

"Oh ho! Now that is the truth!" Richard agreed with a chuckle.

"So, Mr. Collins proposed, and you refused him?" Amelia asked, guiding the discussion back to what she likely held as the most important bit of information. She had refused two gentlemen already, and who knew how many more hopeful bucks would be turned away this season. She would not marry for anything other than love, and he, as her father, would not press her to accept someone who did not engage her heart. Not even for political advantage, though it was tempting.

"Yes. Would that he had deigned to accept my first reply, but he did not. I had to repeat my refusal a few times before he was duly convinced that I did not wish to marry him. My mother..." She darted a glance in Mrs. Bennet's direction. "Was not pleased."

"I dare say I was not pleased," Mrs. Bennet groused. She shook her head. "Such a –"

"Headstrong, obstinate girl. Is that not right, Mama?" Elizabeth smiled softly at Mrs. Bennet. There might be some discord between the two but there was no loss of love.

Mrs. Bennet nodded and sighed. "That you are, my child, that you are."

Obstinacy would stand Miss Elizabeth in good stead when it came to dealing with the ladies of the ton, as well as certain members of the Fitzwilliam family – Catherine for one and Richard for another.

"Upon hearing me called such, Mr. Collins did not think that his patroness would approve of his marrying a headstrong, obstinate lady, and so, he withdrew his suit. Three days later, he proposed to my particular friend Charlotte Lucas and was accepted."

Richard guffawed. "Forgive me. I should not laugh so. It is just that I cannot imagine you following my aunt's edits, and it has struck a chord."

"I cannot imagine myself following her edict either," Elizabeth agreed softly.

Lord Matlock noted the twinkle in her eye and the small smile that passed between her and Darcy, and he knew that there was more to this story.

"And what about Darcy's proposal?" he asked.

"Oh, that is less entertaining. Mr. Darcy accompanied Mr. Bingley to Hertfordshire and, during a walk one day, we came to an understanding." Her cheeks were once again rosy, and her answer was given a bit too quickly. It smacked of secrets being guarded.

His was not the only curiosity that was aroused by her reply.

"Just like that, eh, Darcy?" Richard's head was tipped, and he was skewering his cousins with a penetrating stare. "Something tells me that there may be more of a story there than that. How did you come to know Miss Elizabeth?"

Darcy shifted uneasily. The man was dreadful at hiding things from Richard. It was likely a good trait that he felt uncomfortable keeping secrets from a cousin who was as dear to him as a brother, but it never did him any favours because Richard was not easily swayed from his purpose.

"As Elizabeth said, I presented my offer when I accompanied Mr. Bingley to Hertfordshire." Darcy glared at Richard.

Lord Matlock sat back and waited. He had seen these looks before and had a good idea about how this scene was going to play out. Darcy would dig in his feet while Richard would drag the story out of him. Poor fellow!

Henry knew he should probably step in and end the battle before it began, but his curiosity had been tweaked.

"Was that last fall, Darcy? While at Rosings, Miss Elizabeth said you did not make a favourable impression."

Miss Elizabeth winced, and her mother huffed. It was enough to encourage Richard, who smiled.

"So, how did you, my taciturn cousin, come to an understanding with the lovely Miss Elizabeth?"

"As she said. On a walk. I am not always taciturn."

Richard continued to look at Darcy for a moment before turning his attention to Miss Elizabeth – most likely in an attempt to draw Darcy out. "You did tell me that he did not make a favourable impression the first time he visited Hertfordshire, did you not?"

"I did, but he does improve upon acquaintance."

"I am certain he does, but exactly how did he improve? That is what I would like to know."

Henry watched Darcy carefully. He looked very much as if he was going to come to the aid of his beloved at any moment. Darcy had a strong protective side that was easy for his cousin to exploit. Henry was certain Darcy would not allow an interrogation of Miss Elizabeth, and he was at the ready to jump into the fray before Darcy and Richard came to blows.

"As with anyone, Colonel, the longer you hold their acquaintance, the more you understand about their temperament, and then, they will either rise or fall in your estimation. Would you not agree, Colonel? Have you never met someone and, upon getting to know them, had your opinion changed from your initial appraisal?"

Darcy smiled and relaxed into his chair. It was an interesting shift in Darcy's demeanor. Turning his attention to Miss Elizbeth, Henry noted the defiant lift of her chin and the steeliness to her eyes. Perhaps he had been too hasty in thinking she was too gentle to navigate the ton. He was impressed by how handily she attempted to switch from the person being questioned to the interrogator.

Richard also looked impressed but undeterred. "And when exactly did you get to know him better, Miss Elizabeth?"

"Were you not in company with us in Kent?" Her voice was steady, and her expression did not sift. However, there seemed to be an aura of wariness around her.

"Yes, I was, but what I remember is a fair amount of, shall we call it, verbal jousting?"

"I would call it a sharing of opinions."

"A heated sharing of opinions," Richard refuted.

Ah, this was interesting! It seemed from what Richard was saying that Miss Elizabeth had not held Darcy in high regard in Kent this past spring. That did beg the question of when else she might have had the opportunity to shift her estimation of him.

Elizabeth held Richard's gaze boldly. "I enjoy matching wits, Colonel."

Her tone was cool, and Henry suspected her words were as much a challenge as they were a reply. Yes, he had underestimated her. He wondered just how long she could hold out against Richard.

"It is one of Elizabeth's favourite pastimes," Miss Bennet interjected.

"Did they get to joust in Hertfordshire, Miss Bennet?" Richard asked.

Miss Elizabeth shifted to the edge of her seat, and Henry saw the look of a protector about to pounce.

Richard glanced at her and smiled, clearly enjoying engaging her in this battle of wills and words.

"Oh, yes," Miss Bennet answered with alacrity. "One evening, I was invited to dine at Netherfield and fell ill while I was there. Elizabeth came and stayed to care for me for several days. She did get to do some jousting, as you call it, with not just Mr. Darcy, but also Miss Bingley. You see, it is something she does with many people. She likes to challenge their opinions, and she likes to have her opinions challenged." Miss Bennet smiled sweetly at her sister.

"But does she change her opinion readily? Or would you say it takes some work?" Richard pressed.

"That depends on the subject," Miss Elizabeth said before her sister could reply. She took her sister's hand and held it. She squared her shoulders and shifted in her seat as if positioning herself between Richard and her sister.

"Touché, Miss Elizabeth," Richard said with a slight bow of his head. It seemed as if his son was just as impressed by Miss Elizabeth's tenacity as Henry was.

Lord Matlock turned his attention to Darcy. There seemed to be a touch of trepidation in his nephew's eyes.

Beside Henry, Gardiner murmured, "Oh dear" before adding a "Madeline" to gain his wife's attention and tipping his head toward Elizabeth.

Mrs. Gardiner was seated just a little back from where Miss Bennet was. Her eyes grew wide with concern as she mouthed "The look?" to her husband who nodded.

This was becoming an extraordinarily interesting evening indeed.

"The look?" Lord Matlock whispered to Mr. Gardiner.

"Yes, my lord," Gardiner replied softly. "It seems your son has crossed the line. Up to this point, there was the possibility of retreat from either side. That option has now fled the field, and the war will not be over without some casualties, I am afraid. You see, Lizzy sees it as her duty to guard those she loves dearly. If you are fortunate enough to earn her trust and acceptance, she will protect you with her dying breath. Jane holds one of those spots, and there are few, aside from your nephew, whom Lizzy will protect more fiercely. Watch and see. She will wound her opponent if she does not defeat him."

Henry's eyes shifted to his son. Could Richard truly be defeated by a pretty, gently bred young woman?

"And know that, at some point, it may look as though she is conceding the field," Gardiner whispered, "but do not be fooled." He chuckled. "Not many have ever won."

"She is a formidable opponent in such an unassuming package then?"

Gardiner nodded.

Lord Matlock was intrigued. He was growing to not just see Miss Elizabeth as a perfect match for his nephew but also as a valuable addition to his family.

Chapter 3

RICHARD SHIFTED IN HIS chair, taking up a more relaxed pose. Apparently, while he admired Miss Elizabeth's clever response to his last question, he had no idea that he had crossed into an area of danger. Of course, Henry would not have thought that anything had shifted to such a place either had it not been for Gardiner telling him it had.

"Shall we say, Miss Elizabeth," Richard continued his interrogation, "that the subject under consideration is your opinion about the character of a man like Darcy? How easily do would you say that your opinion could be swaycd in such a case?"

There was no immediate answer. Instead, Miss Elizabeth sat quietly as her shoulders raised slightly and then lowered as if she was taking calming breaths. Her eyes never left Richard's, nor did his leave hers. A quiver of unease skipped across Henry's shoulders. Even without Gardiner's warning, Henry could now feel the perilous place into which his son had bounded.

"Lizzy, Colonel Fitzwilliam," Mrs. Gardiner said, "may I suggest a change in the topic of conversation before someone well and truly loses her temper and says something regretful?"

Unease once again skittered across Henry's shoulders as he watched the interaction between his son and Miss Elizabeth. He was beginning to think that perhaps she and Darcy were even better matched than he had thought up to this point. Both had quick wits. Both were, from all appearances, excessively protective, and, based on Mrs. Gardiner's words just now, it seemed both possessed tempers that when unleashed were impressive – damaging but impressive.

"All will be well." Miss Elizabeth spoke to her aunt, but her eyes did not waver from how they were intently holding Richards. She was most certainly not a lady to be easily cowed and sent scurrying.

Her shoulders lifted and lowered once more before she smiled what Lord Matlock could only describe as an understatedly cunning smile before beginning her reply to Richard's question.

"It depends on the man, does it not? Some men are easily read like a child's primer, while others are more complex – more like a dissertation on philosophy. It could, therefore, be mere moments or days, weeks, months, or even years before some opinions may be altered. So, I would ask you, Colonel, would you say that your cousin is simple or complex? And to what degree would you say he is either simple or complex?"

Her cunning smile was precisely the correct expression to accompany such a rebuttal. It was clever. Richard would have to admit that Darcy was no mere simpleton, and then, if it were Henry pursuing an opponent, he would press Richard on how quickly a stranger – even a clever one – would be able to understand Darcy's complexities. He shifted his attention to his nephew who had been fortunate to secure a lady with a mind that was as lively as Miss Elizabeth's was.

Darcy did not look at ease. In fact, he looked gravely concerned.

"Elizabeth." Darcy's voice was calm and soft. "Perhaps your aunt is correct. Perhaps we should change the subject."

Darcy's uncle gave him an inquisitive look. How had Darcy learned to recognize "the look" in so short an acquaintance with Miss Elizabeth?

"I am not the one who initiated the conversation. Therefore, it is not for me to shift directions. I believe that responsibility lies with the colonel." Her smile softened when she glanced at Darcy. "I, for one, would not be opposed to such an action, but it is not up to me."

Darcy turned to Richard.

"It is easy enough to end this discussion," Richard said before Darcy could say anything. "Miss Elizabeth only needs to tell me the whole story about how you went from creating a poor impression to being so happily engaged. How hard could that be?"

"Harder than you might think," Darcy replied with a small growl in his voice. "Am I to believe that you are determined to not let this go?"

"Ah, Darcy, you know me so well."

Darcy sighed and, looking at Elizabeth, gave a slight nod of his head.

"Jane," Miss Elizabeth said softly as she turned to her sister, "would you and Aunt Gardiner please take Mama for a stroll of the long gallery?"

"Why must I leave?" Mrs. Bennet demanded.

"For your nerves, Mama," Miss Bennet replied.

"My nerves? Whatever has your sister done?"

"Nothing heinous, though you may think so," Miss Elizabeth replied. "Please, Mama. It would be better for you to hear this story from Jane in private."

There was true concern etched in Miss Elizabeth's features.

"Later, I will answer any questions you may have."

"Does your father know what you have done?" Mrs. Bennet was looking a trifle pale.

Miss Elizabeth shook her head. "Only Jane knows, and Mr. Darcy, of course."

Her mother, who had risen, gasped and dropped back down into her seat. "He did not...?"

"No, Mama. Mr. Darcy has been all that is good. Indeed, he has been better than he needed to be. Please."

Mrs. Bennet studied her daughter for a moment before rising once again and exiting the room with Miss Bennet and Mrs. Gardiner.

Mr. Gardiner began to rise to follow the ladies, but Miss Elizabeth stopped him. "No, please, Uncle. I would like for you to stay. I may need you as my witness when I face Mother later."

Lord Matlock's interest was thoroughly aroused now. What had this young woman done that would make her mother so displeased? Perhaps Richard had pushed a trifle too far this time. Miss Elizabeth looked genuinely worried, and Darcy was glowering as a result. Family unity might need some gentle ministrations to be restored after this evening.

"Are you certain this is best?" Miss Elizabeth asked Darcy. "What about..." She gave a quick look towards Georgiana.

Was she worried it was inappropriate for Georgiana to hear? Henry's eyebrows rose of their own accord at the thought.

"It seems we have no other option." Darcy glared more fiercely at Richard. Then, glancing at his sister and back at Elizabeth, he said, "I trust you."

The statement brought a smile to Lord Matlock's face and heart. Darcy trusted very few people with his sister's wellbeing. There was not much higher praise that could fall from Darcy's lips.

"Thank you." Elizabeth took his hand. "However, you concede to your cousin far too easily."

Lord Matlock chuckled. How often had he said those very words or something just like it to Darcy over the years? It was a pity that the young lady had been forced to concede her fight. He would have been most pleased to have her win.

Miss Elizabeth stood and addressed the room. "These are the terms for this conversation," she began. "We will speak of this once and only once. No part of what is related is to leave this room as gossip whether within the family or at large." She paused and looked at Lord Matlock. "Do your servants carry tales, my lord?"

"Not if they wish to keep their places," he replied.

She nodded her acceptance of the fact and continued. "Some information may be withheld to protect those who may be harmed if someone fails to keep this story to him or herself. If you cannot agree to these terms, I would ask you to leave." Again, she paused. This time it was to look each person in the eye. Her eyes came to rest on Richard last, and she held his gaze longer.

No one moved.

"By remaining," she said, "you are, in effect, signing your name to this agreement."

"Well done, Lizzy," Gardiner congratulated.

Henry had to agree with the sentiment.

"Your uncle Philips could not have stated it better," Gardiner continued. "My brother-in-law Philips is a country solicitor, and a very good one at that," he said in answer to the many inquisitive looks which were directed at him.

Miss Elizabeth thanked him and began walking around the group. Circling the chair on which Richard sat, she came to a stop directly behind him. She placed a hand on the back of the chair and smiled as if she were thoroughly enjoying the fact that her opponent shifted uneasily.

Henry shook his head. She had most certainly not conceded the fight. He could barely contain his delight in her ability to make his decorated, war-veteran of a son squirm. If she were a gentleman rather than a lady, he would do his best to convince her to stand for a seat in parliament so she could help him carry his point in the lower house.

"As you will soon understand," Miss Elizabeth said, "there are actions and attitudes that do not reflect well on some of the persons involved in this story, and the repetition of certain events will no doubt be mortifying to some."

"Indeed," Darcy muttered.

Miss Elizabeth drew a deep breath, released it, and began. "Last autumn, Mr. Bingley came to Hertfordshire to lease an estate called Netherfield. Netherfield is the estate closest to my father's estate of Longbourn. It is, in fact, only three miles away.

"Mr. Bingley did not arrive alone. Nor was he only accompanied by family members. He had asked Mr. Darcy to join him to aid him in the setting up of his estate. Shortly after Mr. Darcy's arrival, a public assembly was held in Meryton. Mr. Bingley, being a lover of company, attended, along with his sisters, his brother-in-law Hurst, and Mr. Darcy."

"Yes, you mentioned something about that when we were in Kent," Richard inserted.

"Well done, Colonel. I did mention it."

Richard's lips pursed at her tone of condescension. "There were more ladies than gentlemen in attendance, and my cousin did not do his part in providing himself as a partner to any who were not of his party."

"Again, you are correct," Miss Elizabeth said, while a displeased growling sound rumbled from Darcy. "Mr. Bingley was the only member of his party who seemed at ease and perfectly happy to be in attendance. The rest of the group, your cousin included, appeared to find the residents of Hertfordshire to be beneath them."

Finally, she moved from behind Richard and began to circle the group again. "While at the assembly, Mr. Bingley tried to encourage Mr. Darcy to participate in the dancing. For reasons that I now understand but am not able to disclose, Mr. Darcy was in no mood to dance. He attempted to politely let Mr. Bingley know that he did not wish to dance. However, when that did not work, his dark mood got the better of him, and he made an excessively slighting comment about the young lady who had been suggested as a possible dance partner." She had come to stand in front of Richard again. "That young lady was me." Her eyes sparkled with amusement as she said it.

It appeared she had not been prevaricating at all when she said she enjoyed a verbal joust. This room, and its occupants, were hers. Henry knew it must be, for he was completely bewitched by her story, and he could not fathom that there were any among them who was not. Indeed, his wife and daughter had both gasped at her comment.

Richard let out a burst of air. "Not a favorable impression is right."

"No," Darcy agreed. "It was not favorable at all."

Ignoring these comments, Elizabeth turned to the others in the group. "I do not say this to be boastful, but I am well-liked by my neighbours, and word of the slight did nothing to recommend Mr. Darcy to myself, my family, or the neighbourhood. I am not normally one to take offense to such disparaging comments as Mr. Darcy's, at least, not so greatly as I did. Be that as it may, I must admit that, this time, I was, quite shamefully, unwilling to let my anger go. I looked to find fault with Mr. Darcy in his every move and word, and I spoke my opinions of him openly."

She turned back to Richard. "It was at this time that I became acquainted with an officer in the militia which was stationed in Meryton." She gave him a significant look and then glanced briefly at Georgiana.

Oh! The weight of that small look and the accompanying words fell on Henry like a bag of large rocks. Wickham was why Miss Elizabeth had been hesitant to share this story with Georgiana present. Glancing at Richard, Henry saw that his son appeared to be no less affected by this news than he, himself, was.

"This officer, who shall not be named, claimed a long-standing acquaintance with Mr. Darcy's family and proceeded to relate some very unflattering stories about Mr. Darcy. Against my better judgment and the cautions of my sister Jane, I eagerly listened and believed his lies."

Miss Elizabeth's eyes were filled with sorrow as she turned to look at Darcy who simply smiled softly at her.

Theirs was a relationship that had already known struggle and appeared to be stronger for it.

"You seem to be very far removed from the possibility of liking my cousin, let alone loving him," Amelia said.

"You would be correct, although I suspect I valued his good opinion even then."

"I had injured her with my words," Darcy added.

"It does not justify my actions."

"Perhaps not, but it does explain them." He held his hand out to her, and she took it. "She was happy for the day when I left Netherfield, though I did not know that at the time."

"I was mostly happy and a great deal more incensed at the same time," Miss Elizabeth said. "You see, Mr. Bingley, who had returned to town on business, had told Jane that he would return, but he never did. Jane was heartbroken, and I suspected that Mr. Darcy was the reason for his friend not returning. I blamed him for my sister's disappointment."

"She was not wrong," Darcy added. "I did work to separate Bingley and Miss Bennet. I thought Miss Bennet was indifferent to him. I was, quite obviously, wrong. But Bingley being trapped in a marriage of unequal affections was not my sole reason for leaving Netherfield."

Miss Elizabeth released Darcy's hand so she could turn toward Richard. "Without knowing it or even attempting to have done it, I had, in fact, intrigued Mr. Darcy, but he, knowing my lowly circumstances and his family's expectations, did not wish to put himself in harm's way, so to speak."

Miss Elizabeth allowed her eyes to fall on Henry. One eyebrow arched. The arrow that smote Henry's conscience was no less painful for having been sent so quietly and prettily. She knew that he was assessing her, and knowing that she knew made him feel a great deal less noble than he had when he and his wife had discussed Catherine's visit and had decided that it was in their best interest to acquaint themselves with Miss Elizabeth.

"This is how things stood until I went to Kent to visit my cousin and his new wife – my particular friend."

"Her visit coincided with my yearly visit to Rosings."

"We were in company together many times while there, and although I did get to observe Mr. Darcy in a different setting, which did show him in a better light, I was still determined to despise him." She glanced at Darcy. "You can imagine my surprise, Colonel, when he proposed."

The occupants of the room inhaled sharply as one.

"He proposed?" Richard asked in surprise. "While we were at Rosings, you proposed?" He looked around Elizabeth to Darcy.

"The day before we left, and it was very poorly done."

"Indeed, it was," Miss Elizabeth agreed. "And his timing could not have been worse, for, just earlier that day, my suspicions regarding his involvement in the separation of my sister and Mr. Bingley had been confirmed by your brother." She spoke to Amelia and motioned to Richard as if he were an item on display. To his credit, he looked rightly horrified.

"Because of that information, Elizabeth's ire was already riled when I decided to list in my proposal all the reasons why I should not marry her. I thought that doing so would show her how great my love was for her because I was willing to lay all logic aside and marry her. As it turns out, it failed in its purpose, and it did nothing to douse the flames of her anger."

Richard chuckled.

"When Elizabeth's aunt said it is better to not allow Elizabeth to lose her temper, she was not exaggerating. An angry woman with a quick wit is not someone you wish to have give you a scathing refusal."

Ah! That was how Darcy had come to know and respect "the look" in so short an acquaintance.

"I was quite brutal, was I not?" Miss Elizabeth gave Darcy a playful look.

Darcy chuckled. "Yes, you were. However, I deserved most of it." He looked at Richard. "She vented her frustrations about my arrogance, my involvement in breaking her sister's heart, and all the supposed crimes she had been told about by a former friend of mine. When I left the parsonage, I felt eviscerated and as if I had lost that which was most dear."

"But you are engaged now," Amelia said.

"We are, but it was not a quick or easy path to here," Miss Elizabeth said. "It began when your cousin spent a good portion of that night writing me a letter that explained to me just how wrong I was in believing the lies I had been told and his reasons for interfering with Jane and Mr. Bingley. What my mind would not listen to when spoken, my heart heard in those written pages, and it caused me to, finally, examine why I had been so determined to hate him." She shrugged. It was a melancholy movement, filled with regret. "It was my pride. He had wounded my pride, and I was unwilling to forgive him. I knew in that moment that I had thrown away my one chance at true happiness, for I knew as sure as the spring follows the winter that there was not another gentleman in all the world who was so well-suited to me as the man I had refused. It was a painful and humbling experience for both of us."

And binding, Henry added to himself. Such an experience that made both parts of a couple face the reality of losing the other was the sort of experience that would create bonds that none could break. Neither Catherine nor the ladies of the ton had a hope against the pair he saw before him, and he was happy for it.

Chapter 4

MISS ELIZABETH RETOOK HER seat next to Darcy, who took her hand as soon as she was seated. Was that all that there was to this confrontation? Henry hoped not. How could she leave Richard unscathed when he deserved some sort of punishment for having made her tell such a painful tale?

"Elizabeth was not the only one to examine her actions and attitudes," Darcy said. "I gave my own careful consideration and found them to be wanting. I had an elevated opinion of myself, and displeasure with that caused me to change. I admitted to Bingley my motives for my actions in separating him and Miss Bennet, and he was justly furious with me for a time. I also began to look at people as people and not just owners of possessions. There are many good people, people of good character, who are not of the first circles. It was a painful but necessary lesson."

"Is this the reason you did not wish to tour Pemberley when on holidays with your aunt and me?" Mr. Gardiner asked.

Miss Elizabeth nodded. "I was so ashamed of how I had treated Mr. Darcy. I was certain he would despise me, and I would not have blamed him if he had."

"But he did not," Gardiner said with some force. "He was a gracious host."

Again, Miss Elizabeth nodded her agreement. "He was, and that was when I truly knew how utterly wrong I had been about him. He was not proud; he was reserved and very concerned about fulfilling the duties to which he felt bound."

She smiled softly when she looked at Henry, but he felt the arrow.

"According to his housekeeper, Mr. Darcy was a good and kind master. According to his sister, a better brother could not be found. And according to Mr. Bingley, he was a trusted friend. Every preconceived notion I had held was thoroughly refuted and replaced with the knowledge that a better man could not be found. And that, Colonel Fitzwilliam, was when and how my opinion of your cousin changed."

"But how did you become engaged if you had refused him?" Richard asked.

"I only refused his first proposal, Colonel. I am not so foolish as to throw away happiness a second time." Her eyes twinkled.

Ah! There must be something of interest left to this story. That was a relief!

"The second proposal came about thanks to the participation of Lady Catherine."

"Aunt Catherine?" Amelia said.

Miss Elizabeth nodded. Amusement seemed to radiate from her person. "Your aunt had heard rumours that Mr. Darcy and I were engaged. As you know, this was not the case, but she did not know this and came to Longbourn to demand that I break any understanding Mr. Darcy and I might have. She was relieved to hear that the rumours were not true. However, she found it insupportable when I would not agree to never become engaged to Mr. Darcy."

"Aunt Catherine was not satisfied with Elizabeth's answer, so she came to me and related the substance of her conversation with Elizabeth to me." Darcy chuckled. "The effect it had was exactly the opposite of the one for which she had hoped. It was the first time in months that I dared to hope that Elizabeth would welcome a renewal of my application. I knew that if she were set against me, she would have told Aunt Catherine so. Therefore, after our aunt left Darcy House, I immediately sought an invitation to Netherfield and once there, joined Bingley when he went to call on Miss Bennet."

Amelia sighed. Her romantic fancies had finally been satisfied. Of course, Henry could not blame her for her response. Darcy had acted just as any gentleman who was ardently in love and hopeful should.

"And, as I said earlier, Colonel," Miss Elizabeth said, "on a walk, while chaperoning my sister and Mr. Bingley, Mr. Darcy proposed for a second time, and this time, knowing that he was a man I could, and did, respect and love, I accepted." Her lips quirked up in an amused smile. "And that is when the true work began."

"And what was that?" Richard asked.

"Convincing my father that the man who had slighted his favourite daughter was good enough to marry her."

"That was a bit harder than I had ever imagined," Darcy agreed. "And that brings us to now. Happily engaged." He lifted Elizabeth's hand to his lips and kissed it.

The gesture, of course, elicited another wistful sigh from Amelia.

"That is quite the story," Henry said. "It seems that I – we – may have misjudged you, Miss Elizabeth."

"It is not every day that a – what was it that your aunt called me?" she asked Darcy.

"A fortune-hunting adventuress."

"Yes, that is what it was," Lord Matlock said. "She visited me after she was done with Darcy. And no, it is not every day that a fortune-hunting adventuress refuses a wealthy man. That is what you were going to say, is it not?" He asked when her eyes grew wide.

"I was."

"It was a point well placed," he assured her. "You must understand that I had to do my due diligence to my family. I could not have my nephew being taken in – not that I actually thought he would be, but my sister…" He let the thought hang in the air without completing it. "You are marrying Darcy for love and respect then?"

"I always said I would not marry for less."

"Not even if the gentleman is the heir to your father's estate or a wealthy man with noble connections?"

"Precisely."

"I like a person with principles and standards." And Miss Elizabeth had both in spadefuls along with the fortitude to cling to them. "I think you will be a grand addition to our family. I am incredibly happy to know that my nephew has chosen so well as he has."

"Thank you." She pressed her smiling lips together and her eyes grew misty. How greatly she must have felt the weight of this evening if her success brought tears of joy.

"What was the slight?" Richard asked.

"That, sir, is part of the original contract for this conversation. It is under the clause of information that must be withheld. You stayed for the story, so you signed the contract and must, therefore, accept that this information will not be divulged to you by me."

Ah! There was a small victory. Forcing his son to accept that a question could not be asked or answered would sit as well with Richard as a burr under a saddle would with even the most longsuffering mare in Matlock's stables.

"And being headstrong and obstinate –"

"And perfectly lovely," Darcy added. "She will not be sharing that information with you."

One of Miss Elizabeth's eyebrows arched. "Am I perfectly lovely this evening, Mr. Darcy? Not merely tolerable?" She winked at Richard, who smiled widely and then laughed heartily while Darcy grimaced.

How had his nephew ever called such an enchanting young woman tolerable?

"Very well, I accept that Miss Elizabeth will not be telling me, but I will discover the truth eventually," Richard said.

"I would tread carefully, Colonel," Miss Elizabeth replied. "As I understand it, Lady Catherine is seriously displeased with my marrying your cousin."

"I do not see how that signifies." Richard's words may have sounded confident, but there was a wariness in his expression which spoke loudly of how well Miss Elizabeth had done her job of presenting him with a victory that he was not yet certain was indeed a victory.

"I have been banned from Rosings."

Richard's eyes shifted from Miss Elizabeth to Darcy.

"If you insist upon pressing this point," Darcy said, "I may just let you make this year's trip without me, while I stay at home with my lovely wife. I may do that anyway."

Oh, Miss Elizabeth's victory grew more satisfying by the moment. As far as Henry knew, Richard only went to Rosings to spend time with Darcy and torment his aunt.

Horror washed over Richard's features. It was a delightfully entertaining expression to his father.

"You would make me go to Rosings and look through all Aunt Catherine's books and inspect all her grounds by myself?" Richard's tone was laced with disbelief.

"It does seem a well-deserved punishment for having forced me to tell my tale of shame, do you not think so, Colonel?"

It most certainly was!

Miss Elizabeth chuckled softly. "Let that be a lesson to you about crossing verbal swords with me. Just when you think you have the upper hand and have won." She made a snatching motion with her hand. "The tide turns, and your victory is gone."

Richard closed his eyes and shook his head as if bewildered by the way things had gone directly down the path he had selected and yet had led him to where he did not wish to be.

Henry could not contain his delight any longer and allowed himself to laugh heartily. "I see you have finally met your match, Son. Miss Elizabeth, we have been trying for years to out-maneuver his witty repartee. Well done."

"She may have won this once," Richard protested, "but it was not without substantial concessions."

"Because Darcy gives in to you too easily," Lord Matlock inserted.

Richard held up a hand to stop whatever other comments might be hurled at him. "I will be better prepared for the next battle."

"I look forward to the challenge, sir," Miss Elizabeth said. "Now, if you will excuse me and my uncle. I must go collect my mother and take her home. I am sure that even my witty repartee will not save me from the scolding I shall receive for having treated Mr. Darcy so abominably."

She rose, and Darcy rose with her. "I will see you to the door," he said. "Perhaps I can convince your mother that you are not at fault as much as she thinks?"

Placing her hand in the crook of his proffered arm, she said, "I would enjoy the company, Mr. Darcy, but I know my mother. I shall have to bear the brunt of this." She leaned into his arm more closely. "You know you truly do give in to your cousin too easily," Henry heard her whisper as he rose to follow them.

Perhaps an apology from him for his son's behaviour might do some good.

"I know you think I do, but it is only because I choose to avoid the many methods of torture he can and has used on me in the past to extract information. It really is better for my health to give in a little too easily," Darcy said.

"I shall have to keep that in mind," Miss Elizabeth teased, causing Darcy to colour and his uncle to chuckle – silently, of course, for he did not want either Darcy or Miss Elizabeth to know he had heard their conversation.

She was clever. It really was too bad that she was not able to join him in his governmental pursuits. Unless…

"Miss Elizabeth," he said as they stepped into the corridor and were confronted by her agitated mother.

"Elizabeth Bennet," the woman began, "I must speak with you."

"I know, Mama."

"But I must speak to her first, Madame," Lord Matlock inserted.

"She has not offended you, has she?" The woman's hand flew to her heart.

"No, no, not at all," Henry hastened to assure her. "I am quite delighted by her."

Mrs. Bennet's eyes grew wide. "You are?"

"I am. She is highly intelligent and unafraid to display it."

"And you approve of this?" The lady looked as if she was going to faint away at the shock of such a thing.

"I am not conventional," he assured her before turning to Miss Elizabeth. "Do you read the papers?"

"On occasion, my lord."

"Do you know about the unrest in the north?"

"With the manufacturers?"

Henry smiled. This might be one of his best ideas yet. "Yes," he answered.

"I do."

"What about the conflict on the continent? Have you kept abreast of the proceedings there?"

"Mostly." Her brow was furrowed in confusion.

"Would you consider yourself familiar enough with current events to converse about them at a dinner party?"

"I would like to think so, my lord."

Yes, he would expect her to wish to be well-versed enough in many topics so that she could engage in meaningful conversation. Darcy was the same way, though he was not so animated in his debating as Henry imagined Miss Elizabeth would be.

"What is this about?" Darcy asked.

"I think I can secure an invitation for you and Miss Elizabeth to a dinner party next week. It is being held by a political colleague of mine, and it would be an excellent opportunity to introduce them to my soon-to-be new niece."

"You are not going to use my betrothed to support your political endeavours."

Darcy knew him too well.

"Not directly. But if she were to, by chance, hold to the same views as I, she may be able to influence a wife or two, who would, in turn, help to sway their husbands."

"You think I could persuade ladies of the ton to convince their husbands to support you in parliament?" Miss Elizabeth asked in amazement. "Is that how things are done?"

"After what I have just witnessed tonight, I have no doubt in my mind that you could challenge my fellow lords and persuade them of a thing or two. However, that is rarely how it is done, but a meaningful word to the appropriate wife by my wife – or my niece –" he said hopefully, "is not unheard of and could make my job of securing support from the gentlemen in question a bit easier."

"Uncle." Darcy's tone was scolding, but Henry ignored it.

"Mr. Bingley has relations in manufacturing, and your uncle is in importing and exporting. Both are facing a crisis due to frame-breakers and embargos. Would you not like to help see to their futures?"

"What if we do not agree on what that future should be?" Miss Elizabeth asked.

Henry smiled. She was intrigued. "Then, I will listen to your views and may decide to change my own if you can convince me." He looked at Darcy and then back to Miss Elizabeth. He had one more important reason for suggesting what he was suggesting. "If you attend this dinner and are able to converse on some of the matters about which I questioned you, it will ease your acceptance into society."

Darcy's left eyebrow cocked skeptically.

"I will not lie," Henry said. "I would very much like for you to be my ally in the political realm. I am constantly watching for supporters. However, that pales to wishing to see you well-received by people of importance within the ton, and I know that the people in attendance at this dinner party would be as delighted with you as I am had they seen what I saw tonight."

She glanced at Darcy. "May we agree to just one soiree?"

"One dinner is all I ask. After that, you may decide if you wish to associate with my friends and colleagues and their wives or not. You could influence the direction of England." He lowered his voice. "Many think that females have little power." He shook his head. "I do not believe that."

"One dinner?" Darcy repeated.

"I promise it will not be more unless you – both of you – wish it."

"Do you want to do this, Elizabeth?"

"I must admit that am more than a little intrigued."

"Send the invitation to me when it arrives," Darcy said to his uncle and was rewarded with a lovely smile from his betrothed.

"You are going to introduce my daughter to other lords?" Mrs. Bennet asked.

"And their ladies," Henry replied with a nod.

"Truly?"

Again, he nodded. "I should return to my wife, so you can talk to your daughter."

"Did I need to speak to her?" Mrs. Bennet asked Miss Bennet, who whispered a yes.

He had done his duty. The lady would eventually remember why she was put out with her daughter, but he was willing to bet a large portion of his fortune that when she did, her displeasure would be greatly lessened.

"He is a cunning fellow," Darcy said with a chuckle.

"Indeed, he is." Henry heard Miss Elizabeth agree.

"I believe you may now be his favorite."

Henry chuckled. Darcy might be correct about that. He paused at the door to the sitting room and watched as Darcy kissed Elizabeth's fingers before she rose onto her toes and kissed his cheek. Darcy had chosen well. He would be happy.

"Did you calm the waters, Father?" Richard asked from where he lounged on a sofa from which he could watch the proceeding in the hall while sipping on a glass of claret.

"Of course," Henry replied as he retook his place. "You are not the only member of our family with a keen wit and a way with words."

"Indeed, you are not," Richard replied. "And it seems Darcy has added another formidable member to our ranks." He swirled the liquid in his glass before taking a sip.

"He most certainly has." And Henry was looking forward with eager anticipation to the next time he would have the pleasure of observing Miss Elizabeth take on her next opponent. Perhaps he should invite Catherine to town.

**If you enjoyed this book, be sure to let others know
by leaving a review.**

~*~*~

**Want to know when other books in this series will be
available?
You can always know what's new with my books by
subscribing to my mailing list.**

leeniebrown.com/subscribe
(There will, of course, be a thank you gift for joining because I think my readers are awesome!)

More Books by Leenie

You can find all of Leenie's books at this link

bit.ly/LeenieBBooks
where you can explore the collections below
~*~

Dash of Darcy and Companions Collection

Marrying Elizabeth Series

Sweet Possibilities and Sweet Extras

Willow Hall Romances

The Choices Series

Darcy Family Holidays

Darcy and... An Austen-Inspired Collection

Teatime Tales (Sweet Austen-inspired Novelettes)

Other Pens

Touches of Austen

Nature's Fury and Delights (Sweet Regency Novelettes)

About the Author

Leenie Brown has always been a girl with an active imagination, which, while growing up, was both an asset, providing many hours of fun as she played out stories, and a liability, when her older sister and aunt would tell her frightening tales. At one time, they had her convinced Dracula lived in the trunk at the end of the bed she slept in when visiting her grandparents!

Although it has been years since she cowered in her bed in her grandparents' basement, she still has an imagination which occasionally runs away with her, and she feeds it now as she did then □ by reading!

Her heroes, when growing up, were authors, and the worlds they painted with words were (and still are) her favourite playgrounds! Now, as an adult, she spends much of her time in the Regency world, playing with the characters from her favourite Jane Austen novels and those of her own creation.

When she is not traipsing down a trail in an attempt to keep up with her imagination, Leenie resides in the beautiful province of Nova Scotia with her two sons and her very own Mr. Brown (a wonderful mix of all the best of Darcy,

Bingley, and Edmund with a healthy dose of the teasing Mr. Tilney and just a dash of the scolding Mr. Knightley).

Connect with Leenie

Subscribe to Leenie's Mailing List:

leeniebrown.com/subscribe

Website:

leeniebrown.com

Patreon:

patreon.com/LeenieBrown

Facebook:

facebook.com/LeenieBrownAuthor

MeWe:

mewe.com/p/leeniebrown1

Instagram:

@leenie.b (Leenie B Books)

E-mail:
LeenieBrownAuthor@gmail.com